W9-DAS-192

J305.9069 R69lr

JUL - - 2019

Leaving My Homeland

A Refugee's Journey from

Myanmar

Ellen Rodger

Bibliothèque - Library
BEACONSFIELD
303 boul. Beaconsfield,
Beaconsfield, Qc H9W 4A7

Crabtree Publishing Company

www.crabtreebooks.com

Crabtree Publishing Company
www.crabtreebooks.com

Author: Ellen Rodger

Editors: Sarah Eason, Harriet McGregor, and Janine Deschenes

Proofreader and indexer: Wendy Scavuzzo

Editorial director: Kathy Middleton

Design: Jessica Moon

Cover design and additional artwork: Jessica Moon

Photo research: Rachel Blount

Production coordinator and Prepress technician: Ken Wright

Print coordinator: Margaret Amy Salter

Consultants: Hawa Sabriye and HaEun Kim

Produced for Crabtree Publishing Company by Calcium Creative.

Publisher's Note: The story presented in this book is a fictional account based on extensive research of real-life accounts by refugees, with the aim of reflecting the true experience of refugee children and their families.

Photo Credits:

t=Top, bl=Bottom Left, br=Bottom Right

Shutterstock: Aisyaqilumaranas: p. 25; Vassamon Anansukkasem: p. 7b; Suphapong Eiamvorasombat: pp. 4, 5b, 9b, 10, 12, 16, 18; h3x: p. 11tl; Abd. Halim Hadi: p. 13c; Hafiz Johari: pp. 14, 15, 24, 27t; Laboo Studio: p. 21, 26; Lawkeeper: p. 25t; Little Perfect Stock: p. 27b; Love You: p. 15t; Macrovector: pp. 3, 22t; MSSA: p. 16l; Phuong D. Nguyen: p. 22; Paintings: p. 29; Redline Vector: p. 7t; Aizuddin Saad: p. 11; Seita: p. 1b; Thor Jorgen Udvang: pp. 6b, 8–9b; What's My Name: pp. 18b, 20t; UNHCR: © UNHCR/Saiful Huq Omi: p. 19; © UNHCR/Fauzan Ijazah: pp. 8b, 13b, 20, 23.

Cover: Shutterstock: Macrovector.

Library and Archives Canada Cataloguing in Publication

Rodger, Ellen, author
        A refugee's journey from Myanmar / Ellen Rodger.

(Leaving my homeland)
Includes index.
Issued in print and electronic formats.
ISBN 978-0-7787-3674-5 (hardcover).--
ISBN 978-0-7787-3681-3 (softcover).--ISBN 978-1-4271-1971-1 (HTML)

        1. Refugees--Burma--Juvenile literature. 2. Refugees--United States--Juvenile literature. 3. Refugee children--Burma--Juvenile literature. 4. Refugee children--United States--Juvenile literature. 5. Refugees--Social conditions--Juvenile literature. 6. Burma--Social conditions--Juvenile literature. 7. Boat people--Burma--Juvenile literature. 8. Boat people--United States--Juvenile literature. I. Title.

HV640.5.B93R65 2017   j305.9'0691409591   C2017-903579-7
                                                                    C2017-903580-0

Library of Congress Cataloging-in-Publication Data

CIP available at the Library of Congress

Crabtree Publishing Company
www.crabtreebooks.com   1-800-387-7650

Printed in Canada/092017/PB20170719

Copyright © 2018 CRABTREE PUBLISHING COMPANY. All rights reserved. No part of this publication may be reproduced, stored in a retrieval system or be transmitted in any form or by any means, electronic, mechanical, photocopying, recording, or otherwise, without the prior written permission of Crabtree Publishing Company. In Canada: We acknowledge the financial support of the Government of Canada through the Canada Book Fund for our publishing activities.

Published in Canada
Crabtree Publishing
616 Welland Ave.
St. Catharines, Ontario
L2M 5V6

Published in the United States
Crabtree Publishing
PMB 59051
350 Fifth Avenue, 59th Floor
New York, New York 10118

Published in the United Kingdom
Crabtree Publishing
Maritime House
Basin Road North, Hove
BN41 1WR

Published in Australia
Crabtree Publishing
3 Charles Street
Coburg North
VIC, 3058

What Is in This Book?

Leaving Myanmar

Imagine living in a country where fear is normal. You fear government soldiers, the police, and maybe even your next-door neighbor. You might be scared of being attacked if you leave your home. That is what life is like for some people in Myanmar.

These two boys live in the city of Sittwe in Myanmar.

UN Rights of the Child

Every child has rights. Rights are privileges and freedoms that are protected by law. **Refugees** have the right to special protection and help. The **United Nations (UN)** Convention on the Rights of the Child is a document that lists the rights that all children should have. Think about these rights as you read this book.

Myanmar, also known as Burma, has seen many conflicts. It has suffered through one of the world's longest-running **civil wars**. The violence is often between the government and different **ethnic groups**. There are 135 different ethnic groups in Myanmar.

Bangladesh

China

India

Myanmar

Myanmar is located in Southeast Asia.

Vietnam

Naypyidaw

Rakhine State

Laos

Bay of Bengal

Thailand

Andaman Sea

Cambodia

The Rohingya are considered some of the most badly treated people in the world.

The Rohingya are an ethnic group that live in Rakhine State, Myanmar. They are a Muslim minority. Minority means a small group or part. Hundreds of thousands of Rohingya have been driven from their homes. Those who flee their homes, but stay in their country, are called **internally displaced persons (IDPs)**. Others have left Myanmar. They are called refugees. Refugees are people who left their **homeland** because their lives were in danger. They are different from **immigrants**. Immigrants chose to leave to look for opportunities in another country.

My Homeland, Myanmar

Myanmar is surrounded by mountains on three sides. On its other side is the Bay of Bengal. For thousands of years, people farmed the land in the rich valleys and jungles near the Irrawaddy and Chindwin rivers.

Beginning around 200 **B.C.E.**, the Pyu people—an ancient group in Burma (Myanmar)—established several kingdoms. These kingdoms grew, and traded with India. Over time, other kingdoms and **cultures**, including the Bamar, invaded them. These cultures set up their own kingdoms and **dynasties**. They fought each other for land and trade. Eventually, most of Burma was ruled by various Bamar (Burmese) **empires**.

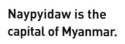

Irrawaddy River

Chindwin River

Naypyidaw

Naypyidaw is the capital of Myanmar.

Many people in Myanmar live in houses like this one on the Kaladan River, in Rakhine State.

Myanmar's flag

Myanmar's Story in Numbers

There are nine main ethnic groups in Myanmar. They are:

Bamar: 68 percent
Shan: 9 percent
Karen: 7 percent
Rakhine (Arakanese): 4 percent
Chin: 3 percent
Mon: 2 percent
Kachin: 1.5 percent
Wa: 0.16 percent
Rohingya: 0.15 percent

Seeking control over Burma, the British Empire went to war with the Burmese Empire in 1824. Two more wars followed. By 1885, Burma was under British control. It became a British **colony** in 1937.

Burma gained **independence** from Britain in 1948, and the military ruled the country. Ethnic groups battled each other for power and civil war began. Elections were held, but the military would not let a government be formed or take power. In 1989, the military changed the name of the country from Burma to Myanmar. In 2015, a new government came to power. Today, the government is not stable, and the military still has great power.

These boys are training to become Buddhist monks. Nearly 90 percent of the people in Myanmar follow the Buddhist religion.

Syed's Story: Home Is Family

I like to tell people about my home. My city is Sittwe. It is the capital of Rakhine State, which we call Arakan. Sittwe is by the sea, where three rivers meet the Bay of Bengal. In my city, there are many fishers and farmers. There is also a big market with many fish stalls.

Houses along the Kaladan River are build on stilts to keep them above water when the river floods.

My father works at the fish stalls with my elder brother, Nazir. We are a small family, but I have many cousins, aunts, and uncles. My mother died when I was 10. I remember when she would play with me and cook me dohpira (rice balls) and pira (a dessert made from coconut and rice powder). That was a happy time when home was family.

This young Rohingya man is at a temporary shelter in Indonesia.

UN Rights of the Child

You have the right to choose your own religion and beliefs.

I am Rohingya. We are Muslims who have lived in Myanmar for a long, long time. But the government says we do not belong and we are invaders. They want to get rid of us. The army and police make life difficult and dangerous for us. They do not let us practice our religion. They beat us and put us in jail, and they take away our land.

Many of my relatives have left Myanmar. They are afraid they will die if they do not leave. I have an uncle in Saudi Arabia. Many cousins live in refugee camps in Bangladesh. Some of my family have gone to Malaysia. But it is hard to find a safe country to live in. Nobody wants to help us.

An estimated 60 percent of Rohingya children cannot go to school because their families are too poor to pay for school supplies.

No Peace, No Justice

When Myanmar (Burma) became an independent country in 1948, the Rohingya were considered citizens, or people who legally belong in a country. In 1962, the military completely took control. The military government decided the Rohingya no longer belonged in the country. They believed the Rohingya did not always live in Myanmar (Burma), but instead were the **descendants** of people from India who came to Myanmar (Burma) when it was a British colony.

The government began to take away the Rohingya's rights. In 1982, the government passed a law that officially removed the Rohingya's citizenship. Rohingya people could not travel freely or hold government jobs. They could not go to university, get married without a **bribe**, have more than two children, or own land.

Thousands of Rohingya were forced to move to camps near Sittwe. The camps are overcrowded.

These Rohingya refugees living in Malaysia are protesting the killing of their people in Myanmar.

Most people in Myanmar follow the Buddhist religion. The government said that the Rohingya, who are Muslim, were outsiders. The government said that they stole land and jobs, and wanted to make Myanmar a Muslim country. Many Rohingya were removed from their land. They had to pay special taxes and bribes to government officials to avoid being hurt or forced from the country.

Many organizations that work with refugees say the government is **ethnically cleansing** the country of Rohingya people. Thousands of Rohingya have fled to neighboring countries as refugees. In 2016, the government began rounding up Rohingya and placing them in camps.

Myanmar's Story in Numbers

Some estimates put the worldwide Rohingya population at

3.5 million.

About 1.5 million Rohingya have fled Myanmar since 1948.

Syed's Story: Leaving Home

Things became very bad. People went missing all the time. Nobody knew what happened to them. My cousin Abdullah was attacked while walking home from prayers at the mosque. The police killed him just for going to pray. They beat him and left him bleeding in the street. After that, my father decided it was not safe to stay. "Soon, they will kill us in our beds," he said.

Even Rohingya children are treated badly in Myanmar.

My father found a **smuggler** who would take us to Malaysia on a boat. We had only enough money for one of us. My father decided Nazir would go. He was a young man of 16 who could take care of himself. I was only 10 years old. My father and I would come later—when we could get more money to pay the smugglers.

Myanmar's Story in Numbers

56,135

Rohingya refugees are registered, or officially recorded, in Malaysia. Many are children under the age of 18.

This Rohingya boy is a refugee in Malaysia.

Nazir did not want to leave. All his memories are in Sittwe. He gave me his soccer ball to keep. It was his most prized possession. We prayed together before he left. He packed water and food for the journey. We hoped it would be enough. Two of my cousins also went.

We heard later that the smuggler's boat was very crowded. Nazir was scared he would drown, but he was lucky. The weather was good and they made it to Thailand. The smugglers then took them to Malaysia in trucks. He went to the capital, Kuala Lumpur. He lives with my cousins. Other Rohingya people helped them get jobs.

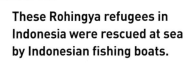

These Rohingya refugees in Indonesia were rescued at sea by Indonesian fishing boats.

13

Where to Live?

Life is dangerous for the Rohingya. Government soldiers burn their villages. Many Rohingya people are forced to live in **internal displacement camps (IDCs)** near Sittwe. Lack of healthy food leads to **malnutrition** for people in these camps. Diseases are also common.

Hundreds of thousands of Rohingya people have fled Myanmar. Some walk to Bangladesh. Others pay smugglers with boats to take them to Malaysia, Indonesia, Thailand, or the Philippines. Once there, they are still not safe. The governments of those countries do not accept them as refugees. This means that they live there illegally. Often, they are forced to pay bribes to stay safe.

A Rohingya mother and her children sit outside of their housing at a refugee camp in Bangladesh.

Bangladesh has 33,000 registered Rohingya refugees. Many of those have been in the country for decades. To be registered means to be recognized by the UN as a refugee. Doing so means refugees can use UN services such as medical care and schools. It also protects them from being sent back to Myanmar. But, even if refugees register with the UN, they are not recognized as refugees by individual countries. Around 300,000–500,000 refugees are unregistered in Bangladesh. They live in camps without services such as water or schools. They work illegally to support themselves. In Thailand, **human traffickers** sometimes sell unregistered Rohingya as slaves.

Refugees have lived for years in tents at a camp near Cox's Bazaar, Bangladesh. They often have to walk long distances to find clean water.

Syed's Story: The Smugglers' Boats

My father was scared that if we did not leave soon, we would be killed. He borrowed money to pay the smugglers. They would take us by boat to Thailand. Then we would travel overland to Malaysia. We would see my brother Nazir soon! Before we left, we visited my mother's grave and said prayers.

With no way to earn a living, many internally displaced people depend on food donations.

The smugglers were rough. Their boat leaked and we were packed in without room to move. I slept upright with my back on my father's chest. The smugglers had to avoid the patrol, or police, ships. Patrol ships do not like refugees. Near Thailand, a navy ship saw us and towed us to shore. The navy would not let us land. They then towed us back out farther and took the boat's engine.

Without an engine, we drifted in the ocean. People ran out of water and food, and began to die. Some were so thirsty they drank seawater. My father was saving most of our small supply of food and water for me. Each day, he became weaker. We slept most of the time. One day, I woke up and my father had died. I was terrified and heartbroken. I had no one.

We drifted more days. I thought I would die like my father. Then, in the night, our boat hit land. We had drifted to Sumatra, Indonesia.

UN Rights of the Child

Children have the right to a government that protects them. The government must help families protect children's rights, so that they can grow and reach their full potential.

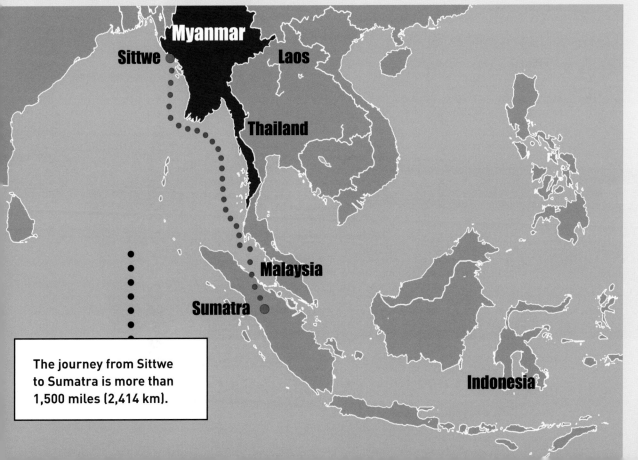

The journey from Sittwe to Sumatra is more than 1,500 miles (2,414 km).

17

Life in Limbo

Every country in the world has citizenship rules. Often, people are considered citizens when they are born in a country, or if one or both of their parents are citizens of a country.

Citizenship gives people rights. These include the right to travel freely, the right to vote, and the right to be equal to other citizens. Nationality is different from citizenship. Nationality describes people's ethnicity, or what culture they belong to. A country can have citizens from many ethnicities or nationalities.

A young boy sells watermelon pieces in a Sittwe IDC for the Rohingya people.

UN Rights of the Child

Children have the right to an identity. They have a right to an official record of who they are. No one has the right to take this away.

Rohingya people have been living in this refugee camp in Bangladesh for more than 10 years. They are unregistered and not supported by aid organizations.

The largest ethnic group in Myanmar is the Bamar, or Burmese. Most people in government are Bamar. When the government denied the Rohingya their citizenship, the Rohingya were made stateless. This means they are not considered to be citizens of any country. Rohingya children born in Myanmar can call the country home, but they cannot be citizens.

Many organizations that fight for human rights say that the Rohingya are in danger of genocide. Genocide is the organized killing of a group of people because of their race, ethnicity, or religious beliefs. The Rohingya's lives are threatened, and their villages have been burned.

Syed's Story: Alone in Indonesia

I was a boy in Myanmar, but now I must be a man. The camp in Indonesia was just a few buildings and tents. I was put in a tent with other children. None of us had parents or relatives to take care of us, so we had to take care of ourselves.

They had doctors at the camp. They checked our health, because a lot of people were very sick. They gave us needles for diseases. I had never had a needle before. At the camp, they gave us food and water. I was given many things, but they could not give me my father back.

Refugees play soccer at a temporary camp in Indonesia.

The camp had workers who told us we can stay, but not for long. It is very confusing. It is not a real place for refugees. Everything is in the open. It is very hot. Yesterday, men came to dig trenches for sewers. They do not really want us here. Just like in my country, nobody wants us.

It is okay. I do not really want to stay in Indonesia. I want to go to Malaysia. I tell people I have a brother in Malaysia that I have to get to. Insha'Allah (God willing), we will be together again. He does not know father is dead. He does not know I am alive.

In Malaysia, some doctors update Rohingya children's vaccination records. A vaccination record is proof of whether a child has received needles to protect them against diseases.

Stateless People

About 10 million people around the world are stateless. The Rohingya in Myanmar make up 1.3 million of this number. They are targets of **discrimination** and violence. Living in the country is dangerous, but so is leaving. Many have died trying to reach a safe country.

Very few countries are willing to take in Rohingya people as refugees. Since their citizenship was taken away, hundreds of thousands of Rohingya have fled into Bangladesh. Bangladesh is a poor country that cannot cope with these large numbers of refugees. Many Rohingya have also fled to Thailand, Indonesia, Malaysia, and Pakistan.

The government of Myanmar posts billboards warning against militia groups. These groups fight against the government. Some also fight for the government.

Myanmar's Story in Numbers

It is estimated that there are between

800,000 and 1.3 million

stateless Rohingya remaining in Myanmar. There may be up to

100,000

Rohingya forced to live in IDCs in Myanmar.

An estimated 400,000 Rohingya live in Saudi Arabia. Saudi Arabia was a safe place for them in the 1970s. But, today, **migrants** are held there in prisons until they are **deported**.

Most Rohingya migrants are unregistered refugees. They have little hope of becoming citizens of the countries where they are living. They are under constant threat that they will be deported. Small communities of Rohingya refugees are in Canada and the United States. Many of them are now citizens of these countries.

These Rohingya refugees are living in temporary shelters in Indonesia. They were stranded at sea for many months as they fled Myanmar.

23

Syed's Story: Brothers Reunited

A man visited the camp one day. He came from Lenga, a city nearby. He brought some used clothing for all the children. He has children, too. He had a phone and helped me call my brother Nazir in Malaysia. I had to tell my brother about our father. Nazir was strong. He said we only have each other now. He promised to care for me.

I wanted to be with Nazir so badly. He found smugglers to take me to Malaysia from a beach nearby. It was easy to leave the camp at night. Nobody really cared. I was so afraid to take another boat, but there was no other choice. My risk was worth it. When I saw Nazir again, I was bursting with happiness. I was no longer alone.

This market is in a camp in Bangladesh. About 33,000 registered Rohingya live in camps in Bangladesh.

UN Rights of the Child

You have the right to special care and help if you cannot live with your parents.

Undocumented refugees cannot legally work. Often, they are hired to work jobs in construction, factories, or markets. But since they are not legal, employers may pay them less or take advantage of them.

We live together now with my cousins Amin and Ahmad. To pay the smugglers, Nazir had to borrow some money. We owe a lot of money to our family in Myanmar, Bangladesh, and Thailand. But I can help. The boss at Nazir's construction site hired me to collect scraps.

Last week, I went to the UN office to register as a refugee. Nazir says it will be better if we are registered. Then, we will not have to hide from the police. Maybe I can go to school when we are registered. My cousins want to apply to go to the United States. That is a dream, I think. Will anyone take us? We are citizens of nowhere.

An Unsettled Life

To flee violence in Myanmar, the Rohingya risk their lives. They walk for days and take dangerous voyages in overcrowded boats. Many of them do not make it to a safe place. If they do reach a safe country, they may not be allowed to stay. In some safe countries, they can live for decades but with no citizens' rights. It is like living in a neighbors' front yard. They may allow you to stay there. But the yard is not your permanent home and they can make you leave at any time.

These Rohingya orphans live in a Malaysian orphanage. Many children have lost parents on the journey from Myanmar.

UN Rights of the Child

Children have the right to be safe and protected.

These Rohingya refugees are receiving food aid in Kutupalong Camp in Bangladesh.

Refugees' only hope for permanent protection is for their home country be safe again, or to be resettled in another country. To be resettled, refugees must be registered.

Most Rohingya migrants are not registered refugees. This is partly because some countries that take in refugees do not register them. They either do not want to officially recognize the people as refugees, or they do not have the resources. Sometimes, refugees are afraid to register. They may think they will be harmed, or sent back to the country they came from.

Also, only 37 out of 196 countries in the world will resettle refugees and give them a permanent home. Some countries are too poor to help. Others just do not want refugees.

Even if Rohingya refugees survive the dangerous journey by sea from Myanmar to other countries, the future when they arrive there is still uncertain.

You Can Help!

It is important to care about refugees in the world, even if they will never live near you. There are several things you can do to help the Rohingya people.

 Visit a library at your school or in your community. Borrow and read books on refugees.

 Research organizations that help refugees. Many are online, so ask a parent or guardian to help you search for them. Some organizations include the United Nations High Commissioner for Refugees (UNHCR), Amnesty International, and the International Rescue Committee.

 Share what you have learned in this book with your friends. Encourage them to learn more about newcomers and refugees.

 Contact a local refugee or newcomer center. Organizations such as the U.S. Committee for Refugees and Immigrants have local chapters. Ask them how you can help.

 Write a friendly letter to a government representative (state, provincial, or federal). Ask them to help refugees such as the Rohingya people of Myanmar. Governments can help by putting pressure on Myanmar to act fairly.

June 20 is World Refugee Day. These young women are marking it by taking part in a rally. What can you do to mark World Refugee Day?

Discussion Prompts

1. Explain the difference between a refugee, an immigrant, and an IDP.
2. Do you think governments should do more to help child refugees? Why?
3. After reading this book, can you give an example of how child refugees in countries such as Myanmar are especially at risk?

Glossary

B.C.E. Before the Common Era; a time period more than 2,000 years ago

bribe Money paid to someone so that they will act in your favor

civil wars Wars between groups of people in the same country

colony A country under the control of another country

cultures Shared beliefs, values, customs, traditions, arts, and ways of life of a particular group of people

deported Expelled, or removed, from a country

discrimination Unfair treatment of someone because of their race, religion, ethnic group, or other identifiers

dynasties Rulers from the same family

empires A group of countries under a single ruler

ethnic groups Groups of people who have the same nation, culture, and religion

ethnically cleansing Expelling or killing people who belong to a particular ethnic or religious group

homeland The country where someone was born or grew up

human traffickers People who illegally move humans for money

immigrants People who leave one country to live in another

independence Free from outside control

internal displacement camps (IDCs) Camps within a country where people go when forced to leave their homes

internally displaced persons (IDPs) People who are forced from their homes during a conflict, but remain in their country

malnutrition Sickness caused by not having enough to eat

migrants People who move from one place to another

refugees People who flee from their own country to another due to unsafe conditions

smuggler Someone who moves goods or passengers illegally

United Nations (UN) An international organization that promotes peace between countries and helps refugees

Learning More

Books

Abram, David, and Andrew Forbes. *Insight Guides: Myanmar (Burma)*. DK Publishing, 2013.

Beckwith, Kathy. *Playing War*. Tilbury House, 2005.

Harris, Nathaniel. *Burma (Myanmar)* (Global Hotspots). Cavendish Square Publishing, 2010.

Mara, Wil. *Enchantment of the World: Myanmar*. Children's Press, 2016.

Websites

http://easyscienceforkids.com/myanmar
Visit this website for some quick facts about Myanmar.

www.oddizzi.com/teachers/explore-the-world/places/asia/burma-myanmar-2/burma-myanmar/
Discover a lot of facts about Myanmar and learn a few phrases.

www.unicef.org/rightsite/files/uncrcchilldfriendlylanguage.pdf
Read about the United Nations Convention on the Rights of the Child.

www.unrefugees.org/what-is-a-refugee
This website has information and videos that will help you understand what it feels like to be a refugee in a foreign country.

Index

About the Author

Ellen Rodger is a descendant of refugees who fled persecution and famine. She has written and edited many books for children and adults on subjects as varied as potatoes, how government works, social justice, war, soccer, and lice and fleas.

E Sp A
Ada, Alma Flor.
Pin, pin, sarabin /

HM $12.75

3 4028 02814 6539

S0-AZD-756

WITHDRAWN

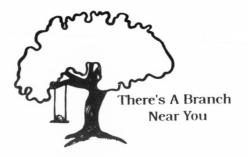

There's A Branch
Near You

HARRIS COUNTY PUBLIC LIBRARY

HOUSTON, TEXAS

CUENTOS CON ALMA

A Gabriel, agradecida.
Tu vivir alegra el mío.
Y a Hannah y Camila Rosa,
mis dos princesas.

© Copyright 1995. Text by Alma Flor Ada
© Copyright 1995. Illustrations Laredo Publishing Co. Inc.

All rights reserved. No part of this book
may be reproduced or transmitted in any form
or by any means, electronic or mechanical,
including photocopying, recording, or by any
information storage and retrieval system, without
permission in writing from the publisher.

First Edition
10   9   8   7   6   5   4   3   2   1
Published in the United States of America
Printed in Mexico

Library of Congress Cataloging-in-Publication Data

Ada, Alma Flor.
Pin, pin, sarabín/ Alma Flor Ada; illustrations by Pablo Torrecilla
p. cm.
Summary: Every afternoon the neighborhood children of various ethnic and social
background gather to play and sing traditional nursery rhymes in the town's park. A
celebration of magic and folklore with the lirics of many of the children's rhymes. A
statement for the elimination of racism and prejudice .
ISBN 1-56492-130-1

[1. Folklore, rhymes, games -- Autobiographical Narrative. 2. Multicultural 3. Spanish
language materials.] Torrecilla, Pablo, Ill. II Title.
PZ73.A28 1995   95-33844
[Fic]--dc20   CIP
                                                                 AC

Laredo Publishing Company, Inc.
8907 Wilshire Blvd. Suite 102
Beverly Hills, CA 90501

Pin, pin, sarabín

Alma Flor Ada

Ilustraciones de Pablo Torrecilla

Laredo Publishing Company, Inc.
Beverly Hills, California

No sé cómo empezaron a aparecer los niños todas las tardes en el plácido portal de nuestra casa, la Quinta Simoni. ¿Sería que me vieron saltando sola "la suiza"? ¿O que observaron a mis tías y a mi madre enseñándome rondas? Lo cierto es que llegaban cada tarde a eso de las cinco, bañados y vestidos de limpio, todos al mismo tiempo, como los gorriones cuando se riegan migas en el parque.

No nos conocíamos formalmente. Nuestras familias no eran amigas, no íbamos a las mismas escuelas y apenas alguno sabía el nombre de algún otro, pero todas las tardes jugábamos juntos alegremente, por un par de horas.

Empezábamos con las rondas. Tomados de la mano, cantábamos, yendo en corro, alrededor de una niña:

–A la marisola
que está en su vergel
abriendo la rosa
cerrando el clavel.
–¿Quiénes son estas gentes
que andan por aquí
que ni de día ni de noche
nos dejan dormir?
–Somos los estudiantes
que venimos a estudiar
a la capillita
de la Virgen del Pilar.

O íbamos actuando, recreando con los gestos y la voz,
la experiencia de la joven a la que llevan al convento:

> Una tarde de verano
> me sacaron de paseo.
> Al doblar por una esquina
> me encontré con un convento.
> Desde allí salía una monja
> toda vestida de negro.

Y movíamos las manos de arriba a abajo a lo largo
del cuerpo, para simular el hábito; y luego, como si
sostuviéramos una vela, cantábamos:

> Con una luz en la mano
> que parecía un entierro.

Luego, agachándonos y simulando la acción de las tijeras al cortar el pelo:

> **Me sentaron en la sillita**
> **me cortaron la melena.**

Y despojándonos de las joyas:

> **Anillito de mi dedo**
> **pulsera de mi muñeca...**

Pero entonces la sangre caribeña y la visión de mucha rumba y comparsa se imponían a tanta solemnidad y el ritmo de la ronda se alegraba mientras todos, moviendo cintura y cadera, cantábamos con entusiasmo:

> **Cinturón de mi cintura,**
> **polisón de mi cadera,**
> **polisón de mi cadera...**

Las rondas se sucedían, sin pausa ni descanso entre una y otra. Cantábamos en círculo:

> **Yo soy la viudita**
> **del Conde Laurel**
> **me quiero casar**
> **y no encuentro con quien.**

Algunas rondas las cantábamos saltando a pie cojita:

> **Desde chiquitica**
> **me quedé, me quedé,**
> **algo resentida**
> **de este pie, de este pie...**

Y también:

> **¿Dónde va la cojita,**
> **que miruflí, que miruflá...?**

O formábamos dos filas para jugar. Mientras una fila avanzaba al encuentro de la otra, cantaba:

> **Ambos a dos,**
> **Materile, rile, rile...**
> **Ambos a dos,**
> **Materile, rile, ron.**

Ante la respuesta:

> **Yo quería un paje,**
> **Materile, rile, rile ...**

Primero dábamos la oportunidad de elegir:

> **Escoja, Usted,**
> **Materile, rile, rile ...**

Luego, era necesario ofrecerle un posible oficio a quien hubiera sido elegido como paje:

> **¿Qué oficio le pondremos,**
> **Materile, rile, rile...?**

Algunos trataban de ser discriminatorios y rechazaban los oficios tradicionales: *cocinera, sastre, carpintero*, hasta que les ofrecieran *doctor, abogado* o *profesora*. Al principio me sentía siempre muy desencantada cuando mis propuestas: *domador de fieras, explorador, trapecista de circo* eran ignoradas.

Poco a poco algunos niños se mostraron dispuestos a proponer y aceptar, por lo menos, *cantante, artista* y *bailarina*.. No creo, sin embargo, que nunca se nos ocurriera a ninguno proponer *escritor* o *autora*.

Nos encantaba jugar *Al ánimo* y cantar especialmente
aquello de que el dinero se hace con cáscara de huevo:

Unos cantaban:

**Al ánimo, al ánimo,
la fuente se rompió.**

Y los otros respondían:

**Al ánimo, al ánimo,
mandarla a componer.**

El primer grupo, con mucho sentido práctico, advertía:

> **Al ánimo, al ánimo,**
> **dinero no tenemos.**

y los otros, generosos, ofrecían:

> **Al ánimo, al ánimo,**
> **nosotros les daremos.**

Los realistas, entonces, preguntaban curiosos:

> **Al ánimo, al ánimo,**
> **¿con qué se hace el dinero?**

y los otros le daban la respuesta disparatada, que nunca dejaba de hacernos gracia:

> **Al ánimo, al ánimo,**
> **¡con cáscara de huevo!**

En este punto la canción se animaba, mientras los dos niños que habían hecho el arco con sus brazos alzados, debajo del cual pasábamos cantando, se aprestaban a bajar los brazos para atrapar al último en la fila:

Urí, urí, urá,
la reina va a pasar.
El de "alante" corre mucho,
el de atrás se quedará.

El atrapado tenía que elegir entre las dos frutas propuestas por los dos que formaban el arco (tamarindo o guayaba, níspero o chirimoya, marañón o guanábana, anón o mamey, coco o mango). Luego, cuando ya todos habíamos quedado divididos en dos bandos, según la fruta que hubiéramos elegido, empezaba la segunda parte del juego. Al ritmo de:

–¿Cuántos panecitos
hay en el horno?
–Veinticinco y uno "quemao".
–¿Y quién lo quemó?
–El perrito tramposo.
–Pues, préndelo, préndelo,
por goloso...
Préndelo, préndelo...

Hacíamos una larga fila, cogidos de la mano, en el lado que nos correspondía. Pasábamos sin soltarnos las manos, por debajo de los brazos de cada uno, hasta que quedábamos todos con ambos brazos cruzados sobre el pecho. En esta posición, a una orden de los que habían formado el puente inicialmente, tirábamos con fuerza, a ver dónde se rompía la fila. No era extraño que, al soltarse un par de manos, fuéramos a dar todos al suelo.

A veces, al caer la tarde, las rondas se hacían más melancólicas. Cantábamos la triste suerte de Mambrú:

Mambrú se fue a la guerra
qué dolor, qué dolor, qué pena.
Mambrú se fue a la guerra
no sé cuándo vendrá,
que Do Re Mi, que Do Re Fa...
¡No sé cuándo vendrá!

O nos condolíamos de Alfonso XII:

—¿Dónde vas, Alfonso XII,
dónde vas, triste de ti?
—Voy en busca de Mercedes
que ayer tarde no la vi.

Todavía a veces, a solas, recuerdo y canturreo:

Al pasar por Sevilla
vi una chiquilla, me enamoré.
Yo le dije, sevillana,
rosa temprana, clavel de olor,
si te quieres ir conmigo
nos embarcaremos en un vapor.
El vapor por el agua,
yo por la arena, juntos los dos.
Me despido llorando
de mi morena:
¡Adiós, adiós!

Y la nostalgia de aquellas tardes infantiles de rondas y juegos, me hace sentir como si tuviera en la garaganta "un pedazo del bizcocho que había que guardar hasta mañana a las ocho"; como en el juego que hacíamos con los dedos:

Pin, pin, sarabín,
la gallina la jabada
puso un huevo en la nidada.
Puso uno, puso dos, puso tres,
puso cuatro, puso cinco,
puso seis,
puso siete, puso ocho...
¡Guárdame este bizcocho
hasta mañana a las ocho!

Pero la mayoría de las veces, lo que ocurría al ir haciéndose de noche, es que los juegos se volvían más movidos. Unas veces nos separábamos en parejas. Cogidos de la mano, frente a frente, girábamos sobre los pies unidos, sin levantarlos del suelo, estirando los brazos y el cuerpo hacia atrás, dando vueltas cada vez más rápidas, cantando:

Bate, bate, chocolate,
bate, bate, chocolate...

O, en una ronda, cantábamos, saltando lo más alto posible:

Salta, Perico, salta,
salta por la ventana.
Salta, Perico, salta,
salta por la ventana.
Antes que te quería
era por el pelo,
ahora que estás pelona
¡ya no te quiero!

No era extraño que termináramos con un juego. Para jugar a *Peces y pescadores* trazábamos con tiza dos líneas en el suelo, atravesando el portal a lo ancho. El espacio dentro de esas dos líneas era el muelle, donde estaba un pescador. Los demás niños eran peces que trataban de pasar de un lado al otro del muelle, sin que el pescador los atrapara. Cada pez atrapado se convertía a su vez en pescador.

O para jugar *La candelita*, asignábamos "esquinas" a cada niño, menos uno. Las "esquinas" eran sitios reconocibles, que además de las verdaderas esquinas del portal incluían los dinteles de las puertas y cada extremo de las altas ventanas de balaustres de madera que iban del suelo al altísimo cielo raso.

El niño sin "esquina" tenía que salir a pedir la candelita. Se acercaba a uno cualquiera de los otros y le rogaba:

—Una candelita...

y el otro contestaba, señalando hacia alguna "esquina" concreta:

—Por allá fumea...

Mientras el que pedía se dirigía a la dirección señalada, todos los demás trataban de cambiar de "esquina". Pero si quien pedía estaba atento y era lo suficientemente ágil, se apoderaría de una de las "esquinas" vacías, dejando a otro en el papel de pedir la *candelita*.

NOTA DE LA AUTORA

Más o menos a las siete, igual que habían llegado, se desbandaban los chicuelos. A algunos los venían a recoger sus padres, los otros se marchaban solos. Unos vivían en las casas a lo largo de la calle General Gómez; otros, en humildes cuartos de solares y cuarterías. Unos iban a escuelas privadas, otros, a escuelas públicas; y algunos, posiblemente, no habían ido nunca a la escuela. Una niña y su hermanito, a quienes traía siempre el padre de la mano, venían ella con batas de hilo bordadas y él con trajecito marinero. Muchos de los otros, a cuyos padres nunca vi, vestían con ropitas hechas con sacos de harina blanqueados. Las manos que formaban la ronda eran pálidas unas, morenas otras y algunas color de ébano.

Y aquellas tardes de rondas y juegos en el portal, me dieron una lección más importante que las de las muchas escuelas a las que asistí: es posible eliminar los prejuicios entre los seres humanos cuando reconocemos que todos somos hermanos, hermanas.

Y me dejaron el deseo de luchar para erradicarlos no sólo en un rato de juego, sino para toda la vida.

Cuando yo era niña la televisión no se había inventado todavía. Había radio, pero salvo los programas de **Cri-crí, el grillito cantor,** a mi padre no le gustaba que lo escuchara porque pensaba que lo que transmitían no era apropiado para los niños. Tampoco teníamos los niños de entonces tantos juguetes comprados en las tiendas. Pero, ¡cómo nos divertíamos!

Para mí los momentos más felices eran los de las rondas y juegos, que he descrito en este libro; el volar papalotes o chiringas, que cuento en el libro **Barriletes;** y bañarme en los aguaceros y poner a navegar barquitos de papel doblado, de lo cual hablo en el libro **Barquitos de papel.**

Me encantaba jugar a los "jackies", y miraba con envidia como los chicos se arrodillaban en las aceras a jugar a las bolas. Ahora no entiendo por qué no le pedí a mi padre que me enseñara, o por qué simplemente, no me arrodillé también yo a jugar con ellos. Pero en aquellos tiempos había juegos separados para niños y para niñas. Las niñas jugaban "jackies", los niños jugaban a las bolas. Nunca nadie dijo que tenía que ser así, pero todos respetábamos la regla como si fuera sagrada. Si fuera niña de nuevo, seguro, seguro que ahora sí ponía la rodilla en tierra y jugaba a las bolas con los chicos.

A lo que sí jugábamos juntos era al "tacón", un juego que en otras partes se conoce como "rayuela" o "cielo" . Dibujábamos en la tierra una serie de cuadrados numerados en los que había que saltar en un pie. Para este juego era necesario conseguir el tacón de goma de un zapato, que es lo que usábamos para tirar al cuadrado que no podíamos pisar. ¡Qué tesoro era para nosotros un tacón desgastado de un zapato viejo! Y, para los que vivían en la ciudad, y no podían trazar sus cuadrados en la tierra con un palito, ¡qué tesoro era un trozo de tiza con que dibujarlos en las aceras o en las azoteas!

Yoyos, boleros, tacitas de barro y muñequitas de papel, que recortábamos del periódico y a las que les inventábamos nuestros propios vestidos, eran nuestros sencillos juguetes. ¡Con qué cariño los recuerdo!

Ojalá tú que lees este libro descubras muchos modos de divertirte y niños con quienes saltar y jugar a la ronda, para que no se olviden las viejas canciones y para que pasen tan buenos ratos como pasé yo.

Harris County Public Library
Houston, Texas